Emily's Cat

S.J COBRETTIE

EMILY'S CAT

ISBN: 9798663383189

EMILY'S CAT

DEDICATION

For George.
My heart is always with you.
I shall miss you for eternity.

EMILY'S CAT

Chapter 1

Village Life

Emily's house was close to a small Devon village where she went to school. It had a small garden out the back that lead onto a vast woods. She was not supposed to go into the woods alone, but sometimes she did. She would go in just a little way because she loved to watch the wildlife.

Emily was six, she had curly blond hair and freckles, which her dad Max, teased her about. When he did, she pretended to sulk, so then he'd grab her and tickle her until she screamed.

Max was a teacher in a private school in the next village. He was very tall and wore round glasses that made him look like a librarian. He didn't like dressing up much, so he hung out in jeans and a jumper. Emily was a lot like her dad. Much to her mother's disapproval.

Emily didn't have many friends and wasn't keen on school. The other kids called her names and were mean to her, so she spent her time reading alone. As her mum was away a lot with work, her dad was her best friend.

They did everything together, they played in the woods, making things out of sticks.

One time, they even told her mother they had seen a monster in the woods. A big hairy monster, that had chased them. Her mother was not impressed, and told them both off for inventing stories.

When it rained they made toys out of cardboard boxes. They camped in the living room with an old sheet for a tent, and they hid chocolate biscuits from her mother. He taught her lots of interesting things about history and animals. He was the best dad ever.

When she was two, her family had moved from Germany to start a new life in the village. Her mother Rosa had a new job writing for a magazine. Rosa told her that their old house in Germany was in the north, which was very cold and snowy in the winter. To get there you had to fly, Emily had never flown in a plane and thought it must be scary.

She was glad they didn't live there now, as she hated being cold. Her mum had her office in the house so that she could look after Emily. Rosa was tall and slim, she had long, straight blonde hair, which she wore in a ponytail.

She always dressed in smart clothes, not like Emily, who sometimes looked like a scruff bag, she said.

Chapter 2

The Accident

It was raining hard, it had been all day. Emily and her mum arrived home from school and they changed out of their soaking wet clothes. Even Emily's wellies were full of water. Her toes had turned white and all wrinkled up.

As they were having dinner there was a ring on the doorbell. "Strange," said Emily's mother, as they never had visitors at this hour.

Her mother opened the door to find a policeman.

"Mrs Baxter? I'm sorry, I have to inform you there's been an accident, it's your husband, Max."

He said, "Max's car had skidded and had hit an oncoming lorry, it was a terrible accident. There had been firemen and ambulances, and the road into the village was closed."

Leaving dinner, they jumped in the car and dashed to the hospital. Arriving in a panic, they had a long wait, before they could see her dad. Her mother kept asking to see him, but the doctors were operating on him. Eventually, they were led up to a small room on the second floor.

When they went in Emily's mum broke down and started to cry.

Emily felt a lump in her throat and cried too, she was scared because it was horrible to see her dad like this.

The doctor said that Max was in a coma. It was like he was asleep, but hopefully, given time he'd recover. At the moment, there was nothing more he could do. He explained that although Max was sleeping, deep down, he may be able to hear them. So they should talk gently, and remind him of nice things, they had done together. Rosa gently brushed his hair with her fingers and touched his face. But he didn't move at all.

Every day after school, they drove to visit him. They'd take flowers and cards from their friends in the village.

EMILY'S CAT

The hospital smelt funny, and Emily didn't like it one bit, but the nurses were always very friendly and tried to cheer her up.

They sat by his bed and Emily explained mostly, about her day at school. As the days went by every visit grew to be the same. Max did not get better. He did not wake up, and her mother was very upset. Things were awful for both of them. Emily felt totally lost without Max, she missed her dad so much. Even though her mum tried to cheer her up, she felt so alone and cried a lot.

One afternoon Emily came in from the garden, she had picked flowers to take to the hospital. Her mother was sitting in the kitchen, crying.

"Mummy, what's wrong? Please don't cry," said Emily.

Emily was scared. She had not seen her mum like this before, even at the hospital. In the lounge, they sat on the old brown leather sofa and her mum took her hands in hers.

She explained that they wouldn't be going to the hospital today. The doctor had called, and dad was gone, he had passed away.

EMILY'S CAT

"Gone, Gone where?" said Emily in a panic. "But where mummy, when will he come back? When will we see him?"

Emily dashed to her room, she buried her face into her pillow. She cried and cried, how could daddy leave her? Her mum came up and sat on the bed, and she explained that daddy had died.

"It is what happens when you had no more life in your body, and the goodness that was daddy had gone onto another place to rest."

"You mean we will never see daddy again?" Emily felt a twisting in her stomach and thought she might be sick.

The thought of her dad, just being gone forever, was unbearable. It was so unfair, why did this have to happen? She felt more alone than ever.

That night was the worst of her life. It was so terrible. Her mother came to sleep with her. They huddled, together under the blanket, neither of them could stop crying. Her mother said everything would be okay. Emily didn't think anything was going to be okay, ever.

Chapter 3

A Sad Day

EMILY'S CAT

That Friday, they had Max's funeral. It was in the local church, all the villagers were there.

Max was very well-liked in the village, as he helped people with their gardens, he loved flowers.

Emily had never been to the church before. It was a creepy, old building. The steeple reached way up into the sky, and a large cross sat at the top. Ivy climbed up the outside walls, and the grass in the churchyard was quite overgrown.

As they pushed open the thick oak door, it gave an eerie creak. Emily shuddered. It was cold inside, the people sat on the long wooden pews. There were big stained-glass windows depicting scenes from the bible. Emily thought it smelt like damp socks.

They made their way to the front and sat. Emily fidgeted, and her feet hung dangling. The pews were very uncomfortable. They listened to the Vicar, saying beautiful things about Max. Everyone sang hymns. Except Emily, she did know any hymns.

Her mother was sobbing and clutched her hand tightly.

She tried hard to be brave, to remember how everything was before the accident, but it was far too painful. Tears streamed down her little face. It was so sad.

As they left the church, villagers came over and comforted them. The Vicar said if they needed any-thing, he would do his best to help. Emily thought if he really wanted to help, he could ask God to bring her dad back.

That weekend, Emily didn't leave her room. She wasn't hungry; she just felt empty inside. She lay on her bed, not wanting to do anything. Her mother tried to make her feel

better by making her favourite raspberry jelly. But nothing seemed to make a difference. Emily missed her dad so much.

Every time she thought of him, she cried, it was unbearable.

Chapter 4

Surprise Visitor

Monday morning, Emily awoke and looked out of her bedroom window. It was a horrible day, grey and raining, she felt alone and abandoned. Emily's mother was on the telephone, talking to Mrs Robinson, Emily's teacher. After hanging up, she told Emily, "This week would be a school free week." Even that, did not make Emily any feel better.

Emily went downstairs and sat in the big threadbare armchair next to the window. It was her dad's favourite chair. She knelt on the arm and rested her elbows on the ledge, pushing her nose against the cold glass and staring out at the rain. A cat sprang up onto the window ledge. Emily was so startled, she fell backwards into the chair.

Jumping up, she saw him, a thin ginger cat, he had a bent ear and a white tip on his tail. He was soaking wet, and looked cold and frightened. He peered in at Emily with sad eyes.

EMILY'S CAT

EMILY'S CAT

"Mummy," cried Emily.

Emily's mum rushed into the room, thinking something terrible had happened.

"Emily, you scared me. What's the matter?"

"Mummy, Mummy, look," Emily pointed at the cat sat outside.

"Oh, poor thing," said Emily's mother.

"Open the window, and see if he wants to come in." Emily gently opened the window, just a little, so as not to scare the cat. He slowly made his way through the window and sat on the arm of the chair.

"He's very wet," said Emily.

"Well, let's get him a towel and some food." Emily's mother disappeared off into the kitchen.

Emily stared deep into the cat's big green eyes.

He looked back and whispered, "Thank you."

This time, Emily did fall off the chair and hit the floor with a thud. She made her way to her knees and slowly peeked over the arm of the chair. Her eyes were as big as saucers.

The cat spoke again. "My name's George."

Emily's mouth was gaping wide open, "catching flies," as her mother called it.

"But cats can't talk," said Emily in a startled voice.

Just then, her mother came back into the room with a fluffy towel and a plate of tuna. Emily scrunched up her face, she hated tuna, it tasted awful. George jumped down, glancing at Emily, and began eating, he seemed to like it.

"He's so thin, it looks like he's not eaten for days," said Emily's mother.Emily thought it best not to tell her about George talking.

Her mother had told her off for inventing stories, and a talking cat, well.

After he'd finished off all the tuna, George began to wash. Licking his paws and rubbing them over his ears. Emily's mother took the plate back to the kitchen.

"I'll be in my office, if you need anything. I need to finish an article for the magazine. You can stay and play with your new friend."

Chapter 5

A Special Friend

She sat on the chair, quizzically looking at George. "My name is Emily. I've never heard a cat talk before?"

"All cats can talk," said George, "but mostly, we choose not to."

"Would you like me to dry you?" asked Emily.

"Oh, yes, please," said George.

Emily grabbed the towel and sat down next to him, gently rubbing his soggy fur. George began to make a funny noise, like a little motor, murrrum murrrum.

"What's that?" asked Emily

"That's my happy sound. It's called purring," said George. "I haven't been happy for a long time. I've never had a family to look after me or lived in a house. A long time ago, when I was small.

I remember being with my mother but one day she never came back. I was alone and had to find food. I learned to catch mice and raid rubbish bins. Over time I moved from place to place, looking for shelter, and avoiding nasty dogs."

"Oh, how terrible," exclaimed Emily. She told George what happened to her dad, and all about the accident and the funeral at the church.

And how she felt so alone.

"I feel sad for you," said George.

Emily picked him up and sat on the chair, hugging and holding him tightly. He made his funny little noise again, they both felt wonderful.

Emily's mother was shocked when she returned. She had not seen her daughter so happy for such a long time. It was a blessing.

"Mummy, can he live with us? Please, Please," begged Emily. "His name is George, and he has no home."

"Well, since you've given him a name, I suppose he will have to stay," said Emily's mother smiling.

"Tomorrow, we can go to the shop and buy him some food. As he's nearly eaten all the tuna," she said laughing.

That night the two of them laid in Emily's bed. George loved the soft blankets, this was all new to him. They talked about anything and everything.

Emily learned all about George's life up to now. He told thrilling stories about all his adventures. Emily told him about school and her life, which was not that exciting at all.

George promised that from now, they would have the best adventures together. Emily was so excited to have a friend like George. As he curled up beside her, she buried her face in his fur, and they fell fast asleep.

The next morning it was sunny. Emily and her mother had some orange juice and cereal for breakfast. George finished off the last of the tuna and said he would wait in the garden.

They walked to the shops, as it was not that far. The village was quite small and the pet shop was at the end of the high street. It was also the local vets.

"What's a vet?" asked Emily.

Her mother said, "It was like a hospital for animals. When they are sick, their owners take them to the vet, to make them better."

Emily hoped she would never have to take George to the vets.

Chapter 6

The Pet Shop

Katey, the shop's owner, was also a vet, as was her husband, David. He was out visiting Mrs Black's, Scottish terrier. "He has swallowed his squeaky toy again," said Katey.

She seemed like a nice lady, she was about the same age as Emily's mother. Katey had long dark curly hair and square glasses. She smiled knowingly at Emily, as Rosa explained to her about their new cat.

"He's not just a cat, he's special, and his name is George," Emily blurted out.

"Of course, he is special, because he's yours," Katey said winking at Emily.

They looked around the shop, for what they would need to buy.

EMILY'S CAT

Katey recommended a bag of 'Go Kitty' food. They needed a bowl for food and another for water, and a large plastic box with sand to fill it.

"That's a cat toilet," said Katey grinning.

Emily gave her a funny look and didn't know what George would think of that!

Emily's mother said that she could choose a toy for George. There were lots, balls of all sizes, sticks with feathers, things that squeaked. Then Emily saw it, a bright yellow fish, it was as big as her hand and fluffy, perfect. She knew George would love it. Thanking Katey for her help, they packed everything in their shopping bag, and headed off.

Arriving home, Emily went looking for George. He was lying stretched out in on the windowsill. She opened the window, "Hello, George, are you alright?"

Getting up and stretching out his legs, he jumped onto the chair. Rubbing his head against hers, "perrrfect."

He looked different today, his fur was fluffy. It seemed as if he were smiling with his two little white teeth sticking out.

"We've bought your food, come and look." Emily's mother had cleared a space next to the refrigerator for the bowls. Emily produced the fluffy yellow fish and threw it at George. Catching it, he sped off running all around the house, it was great fun.

Emily picked him up and hugged him. George made his happy noise.

"You are so kind, no one has ever looked after me," said George.

"It's because you're my best friend," she said.

Time flew by, so quickly, and they spent every moment together. Playing catch with the fluffy fish, chasing up and down the stairs, which somewhat irritated Emily's mum. Still, she put up with it, as she saw Emily was so happy.

In the garden, they would play hide and seek. George hid in the flowers and jumped out when Emily got close. They chased squirrels, birds, and butterflies.

Sometimes they just liked to lie in the sun. Emily tickling his tummy, he liked that.

At dinner, when her mother wasn't looking, Emily would drop some chicken or fish, under the table for George, her mother pretended not to notice. But nights were the best, snuggling up in bed together like two peas in a pod.

The following week Emily had to go back to school. She wanted to stay with George, but her mother said she had to go. Emily made a face behind her back. Monday morning, she kissed and hugged George. He sat in the front window and watched her leave. All day at school she was so bored. Time just dragged.

At half past four her mother came to collect her. She could not get home quick enough. He was waiting by the front door, they bounded upstairs, and lay on the bed, and each explained about their day. George had a spectacular day, chasing a squirrel around the garden. Emily wished, she could have been with him instead of being stuck in school, but at least they were together now.

Chapter 7

Christmas Fun

That autumn passed so quickly. They had such fun in the garden, diving in the thick carpet of crispy brown leaves that covered the ground. Emily would bury herself under them. George would jump on her, sending leaves flying in all directions.

As the nights drew in, and so did the weather. Emily would make cardboard box houses for George, or often they'd just watch TV. Most times, George would fall asleep in Emily's lap in the armchair.

In a few weeks, it would be Christmas. Emily's mother said they should go to buy a tree. When Emily told George about the tree. He said that there were plenty of trees outside, and why would you want a tree in the house! Emily had to explain that it was a special tree.

It was for Christmas, and they had to put coloured balls and tinsel on it. On Christmas eve, Santa left presents under it.

George looked puzzled, he'd not heard of Christmas or Santa. He thought the tree thing was very bizarre.

The following day, they went down to the market in the village, there were hundreds of trees. Well, it seemed like it. Emily wandered in and out of the trees, brushing them with her hand. They had a funny smell, it was nice, it smelled like Christmas. It reminded her how much she missed her dad and Christmases with him. It made her feel sad.

It was hard to pick a tree, as there were so many. Finally, Emily found one she liked. It wasn't the tallest, but it was prettiest. The man said he would deliver it to the house for them.

When the tree arrived George hid, he didn't like strangers. The man scared him. Emily's mum brought in a bucket and some rocks from the garden. They set up the tree in the corner of the lounge, opposite the big armchair.

EMILY'S CAT

Emily's mum brought down the boxes of decorations, and they set about dressing the tree.

George sat in amazement, until he jumped up and grabbed a silver ball. Batting it with his paws and went charging around the kitchen after it.

Rosa, stood on a kitchen chair and arranged the top half of the tree. She put on the fairy lights.

Emily and George did the bottom half, well. Emily hung on the decorations. At the same time, George jumped up, pulled them off, and hid in the branches.

Christmas day, Emily woke up super early, it was still dark. George wasn't amused as he was still sleepy.

They jumped on her mother's bed, and all rushed down to see what Santa had left! Emily was bursting with excitement, there were lots of presents under the tree.

One at a time they opened them up, throwing wrapping paper all over the floor. George jumped about like a kitten, tearing up bits of paper.

EMILY'S CAT

For Emily, there were books, sweets and new clothes. Rosa got a bottle of her favourite perfume.

Emily wondered how Santa knew it was her favourite. But decided as he was Santa, he must know everything!

There was even a present for George. Emily unwrapped the box, it was a blue-collar with a small silver heart. It had George's name engraved on it.

Emily gently put it on him, he looked so handsome. Now everyone would know that he was her cat, and be kind to him.

They played with the presents while Rosa made the Christmas dinner. Emily got a huge plate of turkey for George, and his face lit up. This was his first Christmas dinner ever! He ate so much he looked like a little cat balloon. Emily had to help him climb up on the armchair to sleep it off.

Chapter 8

The Worst Day

One morning a few weeks later, as Emily left for school, she felt a little worried about George. He didn't want to go out much. It had been very cold lately, maybe that was it, thought Emily? For some reason he appeared to be a little down in the dumps.

The school day dragged on as usual. Emily had an odd feeling like something was out of place. As she left school and reached the house, George was not by the door. Or in the front window. Rosa was in her office.

"Mum, have you seen George?"

"Not for a while, I've been working on a new project for work, he was in the lounge."

Emily looked out into the garden, and she saw George. He was lying on the grass, motionless. Flinging open the kitchen door, she ran out to him.

EMILY'S CAT

"Emily help," he whispered.

"MUMMY!" screamed Emily at the top of her voice, trembling and starting to cry.

Her mother came dashing out, "Dear lord."

Scooping up George and laying him on the back seat of the car. They sped off to the vets. Emily ran into the vets crying, followed by Rosa cradling George in her arms.

Katey, took one look at them and dropped everything. She quickly led them into the back room. Placing George on a large metal table, she told Emily's mother to wait outside with Emily.

"Noooo, I want to be with him," screamed Emily, fighting her mother to let her in.

Emily had pain in her chest and could not breathe, and tears were streaming down her face. All she could remember was when daddy had gone into hospital. And he never came back.

"What if that happens to George?

"Mummy, help him," she sobbed" "Please help him."

Rosa had a worried look on her face and held Emily tightly in her arms.

They waited. It seemed ages before Katey came out, she sat down with them.

"I have done some tests and an x-ray. Emily, I'm sorry, George very is sick. There is a lump in his neck, a tumour. It's stopping him breathing. I will have to operate on him".

"No, Nooo, I can't lose him, not like dad," Emily sobbed.

Katey gently took Emily's hands in hers. "Emily, I promise I will do my very best for him. You look after this for him until he's better," she said giving her George's little blue-collar with the heart on it. Emily grasped it tightly in her hand. Tears began to fill her eyes.

"Please, can I see him?" sobbed Emily, "I need to, please?"

"Just for a moment." Katey led them in. George, was lying on the table he was sedated and groggy.

There was a tube coming out of his mouth to help him breathe, and smaller one in his front leg. It was so frightening, he looked so helpless.

Emily placed her head on his little body. Rubbing her face in his fur, "I love you, George, please don't leave me."

The ride home in the car was horrible. Emily was so frightened. What if? What would she do, she could not bear to think of life without George.

At home her mother made her some tomato soup. But she couldn't eat anything. She felt empty and sick.

"Try to eat something, darling," said her mother.

An hour passed, she was trembling and so nervous, at 8.30 the phone rang. Her mother was talking to Katey in a low voice.

"What? What? Tell me?" pleaded Emily.

"Emily, sweetheart. Katey has removed the lump from George. He is weak and tired and needs to rest she will call us in the morning".

"NO!" snapped Emily. "I want to see him now," Emily demanded.

EMILY'S CAT

"Darling, you can't. We will go first thing tomorrow, I promise."

She led Emily upstairs to her bedroom and wrapped her in the blanket. It smelled of George, she broke down in floods of tears.

When she woke it was still dark. Taking George's blanket, she went downstairs. And curled up in their armchair by the window. On the windowsill was the fluffy yellow fish. Picking it up, she rubbed against her face. Tears streamed down her cheeks as she remembered their first day at the window.

Chapter 9

Safe Return

In the morning her mother found her asleep in the chair, wrapped up in George's blanket.

"Good morning, sweetie. How are you?"

Her mother had a quick coffee, so she dashed upstairs to get dressed. They headed straight off to the vets.

Katey had seen them pulling up and was unlocking the door. "Come in, this way," They rushed through to the recovery room. On one side of the room, there were cages with two other cats, both looking a bit sorry for themselves. A small brown rabbit sat in the middle cage.

There he was, in the last cage. He seemed to be sleeping. Emily knelt next to the cage.

Some fur was missing from his neck, and she could see the stitches from the operation. Poor George.

Her voice was croaky, "George," she whispered, "George."

Nothing. She opened the cage. Placing her hand in and gently stroking him for a moment or two. Very slowly, he started to move. He raised his head. "Emily," he whispered.

Emily let out a little gasp!

"George, I was so frightened. I love you so much."

"I'm so glad you're here, I was afraid I'd never see you again," he said with tears in his little eyes. They just looked at each other, it was a special moment.

"He's getting better," said Katey to Rosa. "But I need to keep him here for today."

Emily looked at Katey. "Can I stay with him."

"Emily," exclaimed her mother.

But Katey gave Rosa a pleading look, "Well if your mother agrees," she said.

Rosa smiled and gave a nod.

"But if you stay, you have to help with the other animals. Is it a deal?" asked Katey.

Emily got up and hugged Katey. "Thank you so much for saving him."

She sat with George all morning, stroking him while he slept. At lunchtime Katey brought her a sandwich and juice. George looked a little better, so after lunch, Emily and Katey cleaned out the rabbit. Emily got to hold the rabbit, which was nice, as she'd only ever seen them in the garden before.

Later that afternoon, when Rosa returned, Katey let them borrow a special box to take George home. They gently laid him in it, and Rosa placed it in the car. Emily hugged and thanked Katey again for taking such good care of George.

Arriving home, Emily fetched George's blanket. They got him out of the box, he was a bit wobbly from the anaesthetic. She sat with him on the floor and gave him some special food to help get his strength back. She had to help him by rolling the food into little balls. That made it a lot easier to eat. That afternoon they rested in the old armchair. When Emily's mother checked in on them, they were both fast asleep.

EMILY'S CAT

When night fell Emily carried him up to the bedroom, holding him close. It had all been such a horrible experience. She was so glad it was over. As they lay there, George looked at her. "I didn't believe anyone would ever care for me. Thank you, Emily."

"George, I am so happy. I thought I'd lost you. I love you more than anything." Emily kissed him gently on the head, and he snuggled into her neck.

From that moment, onward Emily and George would always be together. And he would always be Emily's cat.

EMILY'S CAT

Printed in Great Britain
by Amazon